CLAUDE

Best in Show

Alex T. Smith

THIS BOOK BELONGS TO:

. . . .

I celebrated World Book Day 2019 with
this gift from my local bookseller and
Hodder Children's Books.

#ShareAStory

Claude is a dog.
Claude is a small dog.
Claude is a small, plump dog.

Claude is a small, plump dog who likes
wearing a beret and a lovely red jumper.

Claude lives with his owners
Mr and Mrs Shinyshoes and his
best friend Sir Bobblysock.

Every day, when Mr and Mrs
Shinyshoes go out to work, Claude
and Sir Bobblysock get ready
to have an adventure.

Where will they go today?

CLAUDE

Best in Show

Alex T. Smith

HODDER

I t was a sunny morning, and Claude and Sir Bobblysock were busy promenading down Waggy Avenue.

Suddenly, they saw something Very Interesting Indeed.

THE GREAT WAGGY AVENUE DOG SHOW
TODAY IN THE PARK

Exciting races! Daredevil obstacle courses!

SHINY MEDALS!

Starting right now!

(All pet dogs and their owners welcome)

4

Well, there wasn't one bit of the sign that didn't get Claude's eyebrows waggling.

Sir Bobblysock was excited too. A nice, bright, shiny medal would look lovely on his knick-knack shelf, next to his ornament collection.

'I'd wear my medal on my jumper!'
said Claude, doing quite a hearty lunge.

'Oh no!' he cried, suddenly
disappointed. 'We can't take part in
the competition. You need to have a
pet dog and we don't have one!'
Claude scratched one of his long,
floppy ears thoughtfully.

'In fact,' he continued, picking a piece
of fluff from his tail, 'we don't know any
dogs at all. Not even one!'

Now, that WAS a problem.

Sir Bobblysock was just
going to say something
quite important,
when Claude
had an idea.

8

He started to rummage about madly in his beret which was where he kept all his important and useful things.

'Sir Bobblysock,' Claude said giddily, 'you like dressing up, don't you?'

Like it? Sir Bobblysock LIVED for dressing up. So he didn't say his quite important thing, and let Claude carry on with his Very Clever Idea.

'PERFECT!' said Claude. 'But I think you need a nice, doggy sort of a name. How about Sir Dogglysock?'

'Ooh, no...' said Sir Bobblysock, admiring himself from all angles. 'I'm definitely a Butch...'

Claude couldn't disagree with that, so he and his new pet dog Butch skedaddled off to the park, where the dog show was about to begin.

In the middle of all the owners and
their dogs was a bossy-looking man with
a megaphone.

'MY NAME
IS MR JACK
RUSSELL!' the
man boomed.
'I AM THE JUDGE OF
TODAY'S DOG SHOW!'

He explained that there would
be several mini competitions and each
winner would get a shiny medal. Claude
and Butch both nearly wagged their tails
off with excitement.

'RIGHT-O!'

yelled Mr Jack Russell.

'LET THE DOG SHOW BEGIN!'

The first contest was the Best at Looking Like a Dog competition. Mr Jack Russell looked at the dogs very closely in turn.

Claude held his breath as the judge eyeballed Butch all over.

'HMMM...' the judge sniffed into the megaphone. 'THIS DOG'S FUR IS A BIT BOBBLY...'

And he awarded the medal to a
dog called Lady Dainty-Toes.

'Never mind, Sir Bobblysock,'
whispered Claude. 'There are
lots of competitions left.'

Next up was the Very Fast Scamper
Race. All the dogs lined up on the
starting line, and Butch focused on the
ribbon stretched across the finish line.

'READY!' cried Mr Jack Russell.
Butch got ready.

'STEADY!' cried Mr Jack Russell.
Butch got steady.

'GO!' cried Mr Jack Russell.

But just as Butch was about to get going, someone in the park opened a flask of tea and a packet of cucumber sandwiches... and Butch turned and ran towards the picnic!

A collie called Wobbles won the race.

'Never mind,' said Claude. 'There's still time to win something!'

But the next three competitions were disasters.

In the Nice Lie Down competition, Butch lay down but couldn't get back up because of his knees.

In the Best Bark contest, Butch got flustered and sang three rounds of 'Ten Big Knickers Drying on the Line' instead.

And Butch sat out of the Duck Pond Dash as he didn't want to get his hair wet.

The last competition of the day was the
Obstacle Race.

'This is our last chance to win a medal,
Sir Bobblysock,' whispered Claude.
Sir Bobblysock was nervous.

'Just do your best!' said Claude, and
he patted his friend nicely on the head.
Mr Jack Russell blew the
whistle and all the dogs
got going.

Butch managed the
tunnel bit beautifully,

and he wasn't
bad at jumping
through the
hoops.

He avoided the see-saw because it made
him feel funny, and instead headed
straight for the wibbly-wobbly sticks.

Butch was weaving through the sticks in first place, when right at the last moment, his glasses chain got caught around a pole. Instead of crossing the finish line and winning the medal, he whizzed around in circles until Claude ran over to save him.

A bulldog called Queenie won. Sir Bobblysock sighed. He was feeling a bit droopy. There would be no medal for his knick-knack shelf or for Claude's jumper.

'Don't worry,' said Claude kindly. 'I think you did brilliantly. We can do lots of practising ready for the next dog show. Now, let's go home and have some cake. You deserve it!'

They were just by the park gates
when they heard a woman cry:

'HELP! HELP!
MY CUTHBERT'S
STUCK UP
A TREE!'

Claude and Sir
Bobblysock dashed
back to see what
was happening.

It turned out that
all the other dogs had
been having a jolly play after
the competitions had finished.
Lady Dainty-Toes had jumped
on the see-saw, sending a tiny
chihuahua flying into the branches
of a very tall tree.

'HOWEVER WILL WE GET
CUTHBERT DOWN?'
boomed Mr Jack Russell.

'I will save him!' Claude cried and leapt onto one end of the see-saw. Then he told all the dogs to jump on the other end.

Claude BOINGED up into the air…

BOING!

But it was no
good. He
couldn't get
quite high
enough to reach
poor Cuthbert.

'Sir Bobblys— I MEAN, BUTCH!'
cried Claude. 'If you join in too, I'll
be able to reach him!'

Sir Bobblysock quivered at the
see-saw and all that jolloping
about. But he knew he
HAD TO RESCUE
POOR CUTHBERT.

Sir Bobblysock took a deep breath.
He shut his eyes. He bent down, took
a flying leap… and jumped onto the
see-saw with all the other dogs.

Claude BOINGED up once more
and it worked! He scooped Cuthbert
safely off the branch with his beret
and brought him gently back to earth.

'HOORAY!' cried everyone.

'THAT WAS WONDERFUL!'
Mr Jack Russell yelled. 'I
DECLARE YOU AND BUTCH
THE BEST IN SHOW!'

Everyone cheered as Mr Jack
Russell draped one medal around
Sir Bobblysock and pinned the other
to Claude's jumper.

What a wonderful afternoon
it had been!

Later that evening, Mr and Mrs
Shinyshoes came home from work
and found Claude in his bed in
the kitchen.

'Goodness!' said Mrs Shinyshoes.
'I wonder where that medal came
from. Do you think Claude knows
anything about it?'

Mr Shinyshoes laughed. 'Of course not!' he said. 'Claude's been fast asleep all day.'

But Claude DID know, of course – and we do too, don't we?

Get your paws on Claude's original adventures

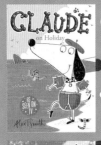

More brilliant books about Claude the TV star!

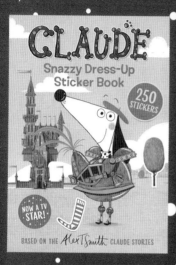

CLAUDE
Snazzy Dress-Up Sticker Book

250 STICKERS

NOW A TV STAR!

BASED ON THE *Alex T Smith* CLAUDE STORIES

CLAUDE
Ever-So-Summery Sticker Book

NOW A TV STAR!

250 STICKERS

BASED ON THE *Alex T Smith* CLAUDE STORIES

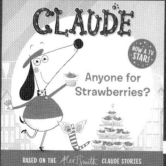

CLAUDE

NOW A TV STAR!

Anyone for Strawberries?

BASED ON THE *Alex T Smith* CLAUDE STORIES

CLAUDE

NOW A TV STAR!

All About Keith

BASED ON THE *Alex T Smith* CLAUDE STORIES

CELEBRATE STORIES. LOVE READING.

This book has been specially written and published to celebrate World Book Day. We are a charity who offers every child and young person the opportunity to read and love books by giving you the chance to have a book of your own. To find out more, and for oodles of fun activities and reading recommendations to continue your reading journey, visit **worldbookday.com**

World Book Day in the UK and Ireland is made possible by generous sponsorship from National Book Tokens, participating publishers, booksellers, authors and illustrators. The £1* book tokens are a gift from your local bookseller.

World Book Day works in partnership with a number of charities, all of whom are working to encourage a love of reading for pleasure.

The National Literacy Trust is an independent charity that encourages children and young people to enjoy reading. Just 10 minutes of reading every day can make a big difference to how well you do at school and to how successful you could be in life.
literacytrust.org.uk

The Reading Agency inspires people of all ages and backgrounds to read for pleasure and empowerment. They run the Summer Reading Challenge in partnership with libraries; they also support reading groups in schools and libraries all year round. Find out more and join your local library.
summerreadingchallenge.org.uk

World Book Day also facilitates fundraising for:

Book Aid International, an international book donation and library development charity. Every year, they provide one million books to libraries and schools in communities where children would otherwise have little or no opportunity to read.
bookaid.org.uk

Read for Good, who motivate children in schools to read for fun through its sponsored read, which thousands of schools run on World Book Day and throughout the year. The money raised provides new books and resident storytellers in all the children's hospitals in the UK.
readforgood.org

*€1.50 in Ireland